*Something **Broken** Something **Beautiful***

(Book Four)

OTHER BOOKS BY ROBERT M. DRAKE

Spaceship (2012)
The Great Artist (2012)
Science (2013)
Beautiful Chaos (2014)
Beautiful Chaos 2 (2014)
Black Butterfly (2015)
A Brilliant Madness (2015)
Beautiful and Damned (2016)
Broken Flowers (2016)
Gravity: A Novel (2017)
Star Theory (2017)
Chaos Theory (2017)
Light Theory (2017)
Moon Theory (2017)
Dead Pop Art (2017)
Chasing The Gloom: A Novel (2017)
Moon Matrix (2018)
Seeds of Wrath (2018)
Dawn of Mayhem (2018)
The King is Dead (2018)
What I Feel When I Don't Want To Feel (2019)
What I Say To Myself When I Need To Calm The Fuck Down (2019)
What I Say When I'm Not Saying A Damn Thing (2019)
What I Mean When I Say Miss You, Love You & Fuck You (2019)
What I Say To Myself When I Need To Walk Away, Let Go And Fucking Move On (2019)
What I Really Mean When I Say Good-bye, Don't Go And Leave Me The Fuck Alone (2019)
The Advice I Give Others But Fail To Practice My Damn Self (2019)
The Things I Feel In My Fucking Soul And The Things That Took Years To Understand (2019)
Something Broken, Something Beautiful (2020)

For Excerpts and Updates please follow:

Instagram.com/rmdrk
Facebook.com/rmdrk
Twitter.com/rmdrk

*Something Broken Something Beautiful copyright ©
2020 by Robert M. Drake. All rights reserved.*

No part of this book maybe used or reproduced in
any manner whatsoever without written permission
except in the case of reprints in the context
of reviews.

Book Cover: Cynthia Tedy

For the broken For the beautiful
You know who you are

CONTENTS

SOMEONE YOU'RE NOT	1
DIE TOMORROW	3
HAD NOT LOST	8
THE WHITE SNAKE	9
LAUGHING AND PAIN	11
LEFT UNSAID	13
WHAT THEY DO	16
THE VICTIM	21
YOU FEAR	25
STILL HURTING	26
LIVE FOR	27
STARTS WITHIN	30
OF RESPONSE OF CARE	33
NOW BREATHE	38
WHAT SHE DID	41
WHERE TO GO	43
PLANTING YOUR FEET	45
THE SUN	50
NOTHING TO SAY	54
BIRDS	59
WAY I LOVE	65
WITH HIM, SHE SAYS	68
YOU THINK	71
MUCH AS YOU	75
THE PAST	77
ANOTHER WAY	82
AND OF LOVE	83
WHAT IT SEEMS	88
FOREVER EVER	94
REMIND US	95
OPEN HEART	98
HALF OCEAN	99
WHAT YOU KNOW	100
SEARCHING	106
DO YOU	111
FEEDING SOULS	113
WEEPING	114
TOXIC WASTE	117
IMPORTANT TO ME	120
BEST ROAD	122
THE LAST	126
PROTECT YOU	131

+ELEVATION+

ROBERT M. DRAKE

SOMEONE YOU'RE NOT

You don't have to be
so uneasy all the time.

So tough.

So goddamn hard
to understand.

Not everyone
is going to fuck you over.

Not everyone
is out to get you.

Or out
to take advantage of what

you have to offer.

Not everyone is like that.
Not everyone is an asshole.

Sometimes
it's okay to be vulnerable.

It's okay to be yourself.
You're beautiful,

baby.

You don't need to pretend
you don't care.

You don't need
to act

like someone
you're not.

DIE TOMORROW

If I knew
I was going to die tomorrow.

Then I would apologize
for all the things

I did today.

I would apologize
for not telling you

good morning all those times
I could have.

For not taking
a moment out

of my day
to reach out to you

just to see
how you were feeling.

Just to see
what you had going on.

If you were okay.
If you were upset

or stressed out over something
you had no control over.

If I knew
I was going to die tomorrow.

Then perhaps,
I would call you today.

I'd call you
to not only hear your voice
one last time.

But also,
to tell you that it'll be okay.

That wherever I go
I'll be happy.

I'll be at peace.
I'll be where I belong.

Maybe even in good company, too.
I'd call you

to let you know
that I'll always be with you.

That I'll never leave your side.
No matter how far off

my soul wanders.

I'll always come back home.
I'll always remember the way.

If I knew
I was going to die tomorrow.

Then I would try my best
to see you

the night before.

Even if we don't speak.
Even if it's just me

passing by for a second.
As long as I could take

that last moment with me.

I would remember it forever.
I would always find myself thinking

about that last time
we said good-bye

to each other.

That last joke I told you
just to hear you laugh.

To make you smile.

If I knew
I was going to die tomorrow.

Then I'd tell you
not to be sad.

I'd tell you to live your life
the way you want to live it.

To not let anything
hold you back.

To not let anyone
love you the wrong way.

To not let anything dictate
what you feel.

Or let anyone force you
to become

someone
you don't want to become.

If I knew
I was going to die tomorrow.

Then I would say today
that I really loved you.

That I didn't really mean
any harm.

And that I am sorry
for everything.

I really tried my best
when we were together.

I really thought
we were forever.

I just wanted what was best for you.

I always wanted you
to have more.

HAD NOT LOST

It's sad.

Because some people
do eventually change.

Some people
do finally realize

the worth of others.
But when they finally do.

It is usually, too late.
Too late to hold.

Too late to love.
Too late to fix things.

To make things work.

It's sad. It truly is.
Because this is the case for many of us.

For almost everyone
you wish you hadn't lost.

THE WHITE SNAKE

When my niece was 14
I bought her a white snake

for Christmas.

She had been talking about it
all year long.

When she finally got it.
She instantly fell in love

with it.

The attachment
was night and day.

She always held it.
She always spent time with it.

She ALWAYS
took pictures of it.

She was truly.
Deeply in love.

Sadly,
a few weeks later

it suddenly died.

She cried. And cried.
And cried

for many weeks after.
We could all relate to this

Sometimes.

At a young age.
You experience pain

and loss.

And you don't really know
what it is.

All you know is
that it hurts.

That it haunts you.
And that through life

that kind of feeling
never really goes away.

It stays with you.
For the rest of your life.

Forever.

LAUGHING AND PAIN

You meant a lot to me.

Probably more
than I can express.

More
than I can fathom.

It was real.
And I felt every second of it.

Even our time apart
made me feel

some kind of way.

Made me feel
wanted and loved.

Made me feel alive.

Somewhat
out of my previous past life.

It was real for me.

I don't know what it was for you.
But for me

it was so much more.

Probably even more
then I deserved.

You were the only one
who knew how to hold me

together.

And I just want you to know
that I miss you.

And that I'm still sorry
for everything

I caused.

I hope one day
you could forgive me.

And I hope one day
we could find each other

and laugh
over all the pain

we've caused.

LEFT UNSAID

You are my soul trapped
in a human body.

My heart.
My love.

And sometimes
I feel like you exist

only for me.

You really know
how to stop the rain.

How to stop
all kinds of storms.

And because of you.
I feel like I am ready.

Ready to feel
all the good things

that are meant for me.

Ready to heal.
To love.

To move on.
Because of you.

I like who I'm becoming.
I like where I am going.

And I am ready
to be myself.

Ready to not hold back.
Because I've lived most of my life

holding

what I have within.
But I refuse

to let what I feel
be one of them.

I love you.

I need and miss you.
We deserve each other.

And I will not hold that
within the back

of my throat.

You bring out the best in me.

And that is something
that should never

be left unsaid.

WHAT THEY DO

Not everyone who says
they love you

really loves you.

Not everyone who says
they care

actually care.

I know that sounds
a bit harsh.

A bit dark.
And hopeless.

But it is true.
In your life you will experience

people like this.
You will discover

people who will
tell you one thing

and do the complete opposite.

This should be expected.

This should be on the top
of your list

when you meet
someone new.

You have to learn
how to identify who's real.

And I know it is a bit farfetched
and ironic

but the only way
you're going to figure it out

is by going out there
and meet

as many people
as you can.

Some will break you.
Some will hurt you

and make you believe
that there are no good people left

in the world.

Which might even be true
but out of that bunch.

Out of that crowd
you will meet a handful

of good ones
throughout your lifetime.

You will discover
a few

who'll have the power to touch
your heart.

A few rare ones
that are worth the struggle.

Worth going through the fire for.
And that's what it's all about.

The more you go through it.
The more you learn

to appreciate the ones
who stay.

The ones
who have the guts

to actually love you.

The more you hurt.
The more you learn about love.

About life.
About people.

Everyone you meet
will teach you something.

While everyone who stays
will help you put everything

into practice.

So before I go.
Remember to be good

out there.

To Be kind.
Not everyone will mean

what they say.
Not everyone will care

with the same magnitude
as you do.

But the goal is
to understand this.

To expect disappointment.
To expect some form of pain.

And to keep the ones
who ease your soul

a little closer.

And one last thing,
try not to be

so goddamn hard
on yourself throughout your way.

Everyone has a story.
Some a lot tougher than others.

Everyone has their own way
of letting people go.

You just have to accept that.
Accept people

for who they are.
For what they do.

THE VICTIM

I'm not a victim of you.

Although,
you'd like to see it that way.

I'm a victim of love.
Of hope.

Of wanting someone
I deserve.

I'm a victim of myself.
Because ultimately,

I did this.
Let's not get it twisted.

I'm hurt
because I believed in you.

In us.

I took the risk.
And I knew the possibility.

Both bad and good.

So it's not your fault.

Although,
you made it easier to break.

You made it easier
to fall into this darkness.

But it's not your fault.
I don't blame you.

And I probably never would.
It is just,

I don't want to be part
of a world

that doesn't have you in it.
I don't see myself happy

without you.

I can't see myself waking up
in the morning

without seeing you
laying by my side.

Or going about my day
and not hearing about you.

It's not in my plan.
It's not in my future.

I just don't see it.

And I know you say
it's over

but is it really?

I mean,
it's been a few months.

And I'm here
and you're still here

with me.

Someway,
somehow,

we always find ourselves
back together.

And that alone
must stand for something.

That alone
must tell us

what we have
is still something

worth fighting for.

Don't you see it?

We're still here.
We're still trying

to make sense
of all the stars

we have within.

YOU FEAR

When life changes.

It happens fast.
It happens without a plan.

This I say
to all the people I love.

Don't be afraid
of taking a risk.

Don't be afraid
of losing it all.

Some of the greatest rewards
in life

come from facing
what it is

you fear.

STILL HURTING

Maybe you're chasing
the wrong things.

The wrong goals.
The wrong people.

Have you ever
seen it like that?

You're still trying
to figure yourself out.

You're still learning
how to heal.

Still learning
about who you are.

Maybe you're asking for
the wrong things.

Maybe you're still clinging
to a piece of your past.

The parts of yourself
that still hurt.

LIVE FOR

The right people find you
at the right time.

When you need them most.
And the wrong people exit your life

when they've run
their course.

When you've learned
what you were meant

to learn.

This is how it works.
Although, sometimes

we don't want to believe it.
But it is true.

The people
you no longer have

are gone for a reason.

And the people
who are still with you

are here
because you still need them.

It is simple.

Focus on the ones
who are still here.

Love the ones
who are still with you.

The ones
you have gone through hell

and back with.

Those are the ones
you need.

The ones who are irreplaceable.

It is true,
the right people enter
and exit

your life
when they must.

But think about the ones
you've had almost

all your life.

The ones you call family.
The ones you claim as friends.

Those are the people
who represent you.

The ones
who know you

more than you know
yourself.

The ones you need.
The ones who you

live for.

AMEN.

STARTS WITHIN

It starts within.

With how you see yourself.
With where you'd like

to be.

It starts as a child.
As an adolescent.

As an adult.
You grow.

It grows.
You love.

And then,
it begins to love.

It starts with you.
With how you treat others.

With how they treat you.
With how you share

what you feel.

How you exchange

the pieces you want
to exchange.

To trade.
It starts within.

From the beginning.
To the end.

Every loss.
Every place.
Every tear.

Every moment of laughter.
It all comes together

because of you.
It all starts with you.

Ends.
With you.

Your world is your world.
Your life is your life.

Your love.
Your pain.

Your sorrow.
Your joy.

Like a tether.

A kite soaring
above your head.

It starts within.
It begins with you.

And only you.

Make it count.
Make it something worth

remembering.

OF RESPONSE OF CARE

Maybe you tell yourself
that this is not love.

And maybe you're right.

The lack of attention
you receive

is not love.

The lack of respect.
Of response.

Of care.

I can see why sometimes
you want out.

And believe me.
There is *always* a way out.

But I can also see why
you stay.

Why you're afraid
to let them go.

Why you're afraid

to start over.

Afraid of putting yourself
out there again.

It's a scary world.
Indeed it is.

But that shouldn't stop you.
That fear of letting go.

That fear
of the unknown.

Of where you'll end up.
Of whom you'll live

your life with.

That fear
of whether or not

you'll be
in a better relationship

or not.

I can see
why you're still hanging on.

Why you're still

taking all of that abuse.

All of that mistreatment.
Shit! You're human.

You're someone's daughter.
Someone's son.

Someone's brother-sister.
Someone's best friend.

I get it.

Believe me I do.
But you don't deserve

to be in this toxic relationship.
You don't deserve

to be silenced.
To be ignored.

You don't deserve
to be taken for granted.

To be forgotten.

You are someone.
You are important.

And you have your own

feelings and thoughts.

So maybe you're right.
Maybe the relationship you're in

is not love.

And maybe
you already know
what to do.

So ask yourself
when enough is enough.

Ask yourself
how much more can you take.

Ask yourself
what is love.

And maybe you don't
know what it is.

But you do know
it is not this.

It is not
staying up all night

drowning in tears.

It is not feeling empty.
It is not feeling powerless.

Feeling unwanted
and unappreciated.

That's not love.

You must know
that there has to be more

to it
than that.

So the truth is,
maybe you don't know

what love is
but you do know

that

it is not this.

NOW BREATHE

This is your life.
You're allowed to change

your mind.
To change your heart.

You're allowed to be
a different person.

To wake up
one day

and not want to do the things
you've been doing

all your life.

You're allowed to love
who you want.

To move on
from the people

who are no good to you.
To let go

of anyone without any kind
of explanation.

Without any kind
of regret.

You're allowed to make mistakes.
To learn from them.

Or to not learn from them
and experience everything

all over again.

You're allowed to forget
your past

if you want to.
Or to stay in it

but you must also understand
that this is not

how you will grow.

You're allowed to change careers.
To dress differently.

To chase different dreams.
To change locations,

even if,
at first,

you're terrified to do so.

You're allowed to dislike yourself
but also allowed

to change those same parts
you don't see

eye to eye with.

To work on them
until you're completely

comfortable
with who you are.

This is your life.

Make it count.
Make your *own* validation.

Your *own* path.
Your *own* way of life.

You are enough.
And you are not broken.

You're a lot stronger
than you want to believe.

Now breathe.

WHAT SHE DID

I ran into a reader of mine
at a bookstore.

I was trying to see
if that store

 carried my books.
They had one.

The one,
Beautiful Chaos.

The one that set
this whole thing on fire.

The one
that gave me life.

A second chance.

I held it in my hand
and stared at the cover.

And a girl snuck up on me.

"He's great.
I would totally buy it," she said.

I smiled because
I didn't expect that.

"Yeah I have to check him out," I replied.

"Yeah. I recommend him
to all my friends.

I hope he never stops writing.

He's gotten me out
of so many dark places."

She said,
as she walked off into another isle.

And just like that.

She is gone.
And she saves my life

for another night.

Without really knowing
who I am

or what
she has done.

WHERE TO GO

It's not
that you can't make up

your mind
on what to do.

On where to go.
Whether you stay

or don't.

Whether you move on
or hold the pain inside.

You know what you deserve
but you keep blaming yourself

for changing your mind.

For not trusting
what you feel.

It's a hard position to be in.
But the truth is,

you need to follow
your heart.

You need to trust it.

You can't solve everything
with reasoning and logic.

Sometimes
those things won't work.

And sometimes
they'll lead you nowhere.

Follow your heart
when your mind isn't clear.

Follow your feelings
when there is doubt.

When there is more
than you could handle.

Follow your heart.
Don't think about it.

Do what you must.
Trust what you feel.

Never regret where your heart
takes you.

You might just get
what you deserve.

PLANTING YOUR FEET

Move on.
But not just from the people

who have hurt you.

But from your past.
From anything that makes you

question your worth.

From anything that makes you
question what you feel.

What's true
to your heart.

Move on.

But not just for the sake
of yourself.

But for the sake
of others.

To lead by example.
To let the people you love

know

that they, too,
can move on themselves.

That

they, too,
can follow where their hearts
lead them.

Move on.

But do it
for the right reasons.

Do it
because you feel the need to

in your gut.
In your soul.
In your heart.

Do it because
it just feels right.

Move on.
And do it freely.

Do it without regret.
Without holding a grudge.

Without revenge.

Without pain
or any kind of resentment.

Move on.

Because you must.
Because it's the only way

to let go.

The only way
to learn what you're made of.

To see
what your limits are.

What the edge
of yourself holds.

Move on.

Because you feel it
in your soul.

Because that's what it takes
to grow up.

To be
where you want to be.

To become

who you want to become.

Move on
and never look back.

Never live where it once hurt.
Never breathe

where there's no oxygen
to inhale.

Never grow
where you can't plant your feet.

And never run
where you don't know

your own heart.

Move on.
Just do it.
Move on.

It's okay to do so.

Move on.

There are so many things
to search for.

Never hold on

to what hurts.

To what brings you further
away

from what
you love.

THE SUN

Maybe it's not your fault.

And maybe what happened
between the two of you

was something
you didn't anticipate.

Something
you didn't provoke.

But the older you get.
The more you realize

how none of that
really matters.

The older you get.
The more you understand

how bad things
are meant to happen.

And how there are probably
a few more

waiting to happen.
It's unavoidable.

Pain is unavoidable.

The emptiness.
And the numbness.

All unavoidable.

So maybe you got your heartbroken.
Maybe you thought

it was the end
of the world.

The end
of your love life.

Well, that's okay.
Shit happens.

You live.
You learn.

And sometimes you go through
the same ordeal

more than once.
And to be honest,

that's okay too.

You heal.

You grow.

And one day
you end up discovering

what's important.
What really makes you tick.

What and who
make you feel alive.

And that's what
makes it all worth it.

What makes it
all count.

You go through a handful
of terrible things

but hold on to
that one thing

that gives you breath.
That makes your soul shiver.

That speaks to you
when nothing else seems to.

You'll learn to live

for these moments.

And that's a wonderful thing
to know.

Because that's how
you'll elevate.

That's how you'll become
brighter

than the sun.

NOTHING TO SAY

That's the thing.

You tell me to be myself
but sometimes

I don't know
who I am.

You tell me to follow
my heart

but sometimes
I don't know what to feel.

You tell me to let go
but sometimes

I don't even know
what it is

I'm holding on to.
I don't even know

what it is
that's really bothering me.

Is it my own darkness?
My own doubt?

My own self-esteem—digging
me deeper...

I can't even say
what it is.

Because I don't know.

So please,
don't tell me what to do.

Or what
I should be doing

to help myself feel better—to
help me find

what's missing.
Because I'm pretty sure

you're in the same position
as I am.

I'm pretty sure
you're just as lost.

Just as confused.
Just as broken.

Empty.
Fragile.

And sensitive
about your own shit
sometimes.

And I'm pretty sure
you don't have all the answers...

I'm Pretty sure
you don't even know

what questions to ask
as well.

So please.

Don't tell me what's wrong with me.
Don't tell me

how to fill this void—this darkness.
Just sit here with me.

Quietly if you must.
That's what I really

fucking need right now.

A friend.
Not a lecture.

Time with someone
who genuinely understands.

Not someone
who's going to take advantage

of my situation.

I need someone
who feels just as deeply

as I do.

Not someone
who's going to say

a myriad of things
they don't mean.

I need someone
who could show me

that I am capable
of saving myself.

Someone I could trust.

Someone I need
when I feel like

I can no longer go on.
Just be there for me.

That is all I ask.

And listen to me...

Even when
I have nothing

to say.

BIRDS

Almost everyone knows
what it's like.

Believe me,
a lot of people

have been there.

A lot of people
are feeling exactly

what you're feeling.

So you're never quite alone.
You're never quite

singled out
into feeling something

no one
has ever felt before.

There's always someone
who understands.

Always someone
who's been through what

you've been through.

Who has survived
the exact same hardship

and can tell you
from experience

that things do get better
with time.

That things
do heal.

That people do eventually
learn

how to move on.

How to actually put the past
behind them.

So there's no reason for you
to believe

that you're alone.

No reason to feel
like no one is listening.

Like no one fully understands

what the heaviness is like
that burdens you.

There's always someone
to talk to.

There's always someone
willing to listen.

To take it all in
and tell you

how everything will work itself out.
How everything

is going to be
okay in the end.

There's always someone out there
willing to give you

the right advice.
The right sign

you're looking for.
The right words

to touch your soul.
And the right feelings
to ease the ache

in your heart.

So you should never
close yourself up.

We are not meant
to be caged in.

We are not meant
to run away

from our problems.
To ignore the matters

of the heart.

We are not meant
to be alone.

Although,
sometimes we feel alone

but those are the times
when we need someone

the most.

When we need to be held
the hardest.

Loved the deepest,

you know?

So please.

Don't ever feel
like you're the last person

on this earth.

Don't ever feel
like you have no one
to vent to.

There are so many
people out there.

So many people
willing to give you

a piece of their heart.

So many people
who are searching-looking

for the right person
to pour themselves into.

We are not meant
to hold ourselves back.

We are meant

to share what we love.

Share what we fear.
And somewhere in-between

we are meant
to find the people

who give us the courage
to keep going.

The ones
who give us hope.

The ones
who make us feel

less alone.

WAY I LOVE

It is almost impossible
for me

not to fall deeply
into people.

The more I care.
The more it hurts.

The more I give.
The less I receive.

I've become
so used to this.

That I have forgotten
what it is like to be loved.

To be cared for.

I'm so used to
watching out for others

that I don't know
what to do

when someone wants to
hold my heart.

When someone wants to
caress my soul.

I don't know how to react.

I don't know
what to do with a smile.

What to do
with a kiss.

What to do
with a flower.

What to do
with a kind gesture.

With some kind of sympathy
toward me.

It's strange.
I know.

But I guess
in a lot of ways,

you can say
that I'm a sucker for the people

I care about.
The people I need

in my life.

Even people
I don't know sometimes

get the best of me.

That's just
the way I am.

That's just
the way I love.

WITH HIM, SHE SAYS

"Why do I continue
to try

with my ex,
knowing

I have no future
with him," she says.

"Because
you have a heart

full of stars—full of hope.

Because
the way you love
is too much.

Too much
for your own good.

Too much
for you to handle.

Too much for you
to know

what to do with it—for

you to know
who to share it with.

Because you believe
in people.

In change.
In the spark

of goodness they have.
Even if

it's just a little bit.

Because you want
to see them happy.

Because you want
to save them

no matter what.

No matter how far off
the deep end

they go.

Because you want
to make sure

they make it back

to the shore.

Because you want
to make sure

they don't drown—they
don't lose themselves

in the transition.

That's why.

That's why you keep
giving them chance

after chance.

That's why you keep
letting them back in—apology
after apology.

That's how big
your heart is.

How deep your love is.

You give them everything
you've got.

Even when you know
it won't work out."

YOU THINK

Stop looking for validation
for the way you love.

Stop looking for your past
in everyone you meet.

Stop asking
the questions you already know

the answers to.

Stop chasing
what you know

you don't deserve.

Stop putting yourself
in tough situations.

Stop giving your love
to the people

who don't appreciate it.
To the people

who don't give a fuck
about you.

Stop apologizing
for the things

you can't control.

For your mistakes.
For your feelings.

For the way you love.

Stop putting yourself down.
Stop believing

in your self-doubt.
In things

that kill
your self-esteem.

In things
that devour

your self-confidence.

Stop disliking who you are.
Stop trying to be

someone you're not.

Stop trying to impress the crowd.
The people who don't know

what to feel.

What to think.
What to do.

Stop trying to follow
someone else's dream.

Someone else's perception of you.
Someone else's way

of life.

Stop trying to make
everyone happy.

And stop holding on to
the things that weigh you down.

You don't need
that kind of negativity.

You don't deserve
that kind of breaking.

You're better than that.
You know it

and I know it.

You carry the whole

goddamn universe
in your soul.

Stop following black holes.
Stop following

your own darkness.

Stop giving in
to the things

to the people
and galaxies that will crush you.

You're so much better
than you think.

MUCH AS YOU

Some of the most
important people

in your life
will be the hardest

to love.

Always remember that.

Never give up
on anyone who's willing

to give up
everything for you.

Never turn your back.

Sometimes
they need you more

than you need them.

Sometimes
they need to be saved.

Need to be held.

Need to be listened to.

Cared for.
And loved.

Just as much
as you.

THE PAST

You don't have to
compete with anyone.

You don't have to
feel a certain way

because the person you once loved
is now with someone new.

No one is the same.
No one feels

and thinks the same way
as you do.

No one feels
and loves two different people

the same.

So you guys broke up.
And now you feel

resentment towards him.
Toward her

because you know
she has brought out

a different side of him.

Because he is doing things
you wanted him to do

with you.

But you can't put
all of that on him.

People bring out
different sides of them.

Sometimes
without them even knowing
at all.

And you have to ask yourself,
would you

do the same things
with your new lover

as you did
with your previous one?

Of course not.

So why the shade?
Why the constant disapproval

of your ex's new relationship?

Why the constant shaming
of someone you once loved.

Shouldn't you be
happy for them?

Wouldn't you want him
to be okay?

To move on as well?
So it didn't work out.

Big deal.

You didn't get
what you wanted.

It happens.

But don't hate her
for making him happy.

And don't hate him
for finding something in her

that maybe
he didn't see in you.

It's okay

for people to find
happiness without each other.

It's okay
for things to sometimes

fall apart.

For two people
to spend years together

and become
complete strangers suddenly.

Things like that
happen all of the time.

Things like that
are unavoidable.

So maybe you got
your heart broken.

And maybe you feel like
you invested much more

than you anticipated.

Well, that's okay too.

But don't hate him

because it didn't work out.
And don't hate her

because she makes him happy.

You're better than that.
And like I said,

things happen.
People break up.

They find someone new
and forget about old flames.

It happens.

It's called growing up.
It's called

letting go of the past
and moving on.

ANOTHER WAY

I remember
the way you left.

The way you didn't care.
The way you left me hanging.

Several years
have passed.

And now
you want to give me
your attention.

Your love.

I remember
when you had mine.

When you let it go.

Some things don't change.
I remember who you are.

And that is enough for me
to look

the other way.

AND OF LOVE

Allow yourself
to be loved.

I know the fear
of getting hurt again

is in the back
of your heart.

But you have to allow yourself
to be loved again.

To be cared for
and held.

You are not meant
to be alone.

Not meant
to walk away

from good people—loving
people.

You are not meant
to be unkind to yourself.

Not meant

to hold yourself back
from something you want.

You deserve long walks
and even longer nights

with someone
you love.

You deserve magic.
You deserve to find it

in someone
you least expect.

You deserve someone
who isn't afraid to stay.

Who isn't all talk.

Someone who actually
shows you how much

they need you.

Especially, every moment
they have a chance to.

You deserve to be remembered.
To be called

in the middle of the night.
To be told

how much you're missed.

How much you're appreciated.
Loved and needed.

You deserve to feel special.
Because you are.

You deserve unplanned laughter.
Unplanned moments that are meant

to take your breath away.

You deserve
all of these things and more.

But you must
allow them to *happen.*

You must let yourself go.
Not take everything too serious,

you know?

You deserve
the whole goddamn universe.

But only

if you want it.

Only
if you see yourself

at the center of it all.
At the center
of what speaks to you.

You deserve to be happy.
Really fucking happy.

So allow yourself to be happy.

To find it,
even if you're terrified
of the journey.

Being afraid to love
is one thing

but not giving yourself
another try

is something else.

Don't shut yourself out.
Don't let the people

who've hurt you

shape your future.

Don't let the past
interfere with your heart.

With what you feel.

You deserve
so much more
than you think.

You deserve to live.
Deserve to move on.

And love.

That is all.

WHAT IT SEEMS

Sometimes love
isn't what it seems.

Sometimes things
don't turn out.

Things don't happen
the way you want them to.

Sometimes life
takes you to a place

you never imagined.

Sometimes good things hurt.
Sometimes people enter your life

to heal you.
Or to break you.

To teach you a lesson.

Something you
cannot learn in school.

Sometimes you get
what you want.
Only to discover

that it is *not* what you
wanted after all.

Sometimes the love
of your life

passes you by.

And sometimes
the one you end up with

is enough
to make you smile.

Enough
to make your life good.

Worth it, you know?

Sometimes you are the poem.
And the words

are a reflection
of what you see

or feel
within yourself.

Sometimes you want
someone to stay.

And sometimes
when they do,

you find yourself moving on—leaving
them far behind.

Sometimes you're the one
who causes the pain.

While other times
you find yourself

on the brink of shattering.

In the mercy
of someone else's love.

Sometimes you get
a second chance

and sometimes
you miss it.

You don't even notice it
to make the best of it.

Sometimes your friends
know more about you

then you know
about yourself.

And sometimes
you have more real friends
than you think.

Sometimes you find yourself
feeling alone.

While other times
you're going to wish

you had solitude
on your side.

Sometimes you find love
at the wrong time.

And sometimes you find it
in the strangest of places.

We can go on
about everything.

Go on
about how your life

should turn out.
On how it shouldn't.

On what to avoid
and what to hold on to.

But what's the difference.
What good would that do?

Things happen.
Both bad and good.

You just have to realize
how sometimes

some things will work out
in your favor.

While other times
they won't.

Sometimes you get
what you asked for.

And sometimes you get more.
When it is all said and done

every loss
is a blessing.

Every moment
is beautiful.

And everyone you meet,
you will meet for a reason.

So take this with you.

Remember it
when you must.

*"You must learn
to welcome everything*

that is meant for you.

*Learn to let go
when you must let go.*

*And hold on
to the things worth keeping.*

*In the end,
they'll make you who you are.*

*They'll teach you more
about love*

than you think."

FOREVER EVER

What hurts.
What never heals.

What follows you.
What never lets you go.

Lingers
somewhere in the back
of your throat.

In the back
of your heart.

Forever.

REMIND US

We search for things
that speak to us.

For things
we emotionally connect to.

For things
that make us feel alive.

Things that make us feel
closer to one another.

We relate in this fashion.

Through memory.
Through laughter.
Through pain.

I feel what you feel.
You feel what I feel.

And somewhere in between
we find peace.

We find a calmness
that cannot be expressed with words.

Whether it be

a video I saw online.

A poem I read in a magazine.
A film I watched

over the weekend.

We search the searched
for things

that speak to us.

Things that relate
to what we feel inside.

This is how we communicate.
How we are given

some kind of importance.
And then

we share it with the world.

Whether it be
through our friends.

Through our social media.
Through our thoughts and feelings.

We share what we love
with the *people we love.*

And somehow
that gives us validation.

That gives us
a sense of being appreciated.

Of being noticed.

That's enough for us
to keep going.

To keep searching.
To keep sharing what represents us

the most.

We search for things
that speak to us.

For things
we are emotionally connected to.

To share it.
In hopes

for someone to take time

out of their day
and remind us
why we're not alone.

OPEN HEART

It is a terrifying thing
to go through.

To have your heart open
while knowing

the one you love
has let you go.

In order
to love

someone else.

HALF OCEAN

I do not know
what has got a hold of me.

I'm half the flower
I used to be.

Half ocean.
Half moon.

Half sky.

I do not know what has happened.

Sometimes I feel
more lost than before.

More empty.
More lifeless.

There's an earthquake
going on inside of me.

And it is shifting
everything I know.

*This is what it must feel
like to be in love.*

WHAT YOU KNOW

It's okay
if you got your heart broken.

It's okay
if they left you.

If they left you feeling
alone and unwanted.

If they left you
with an even bigger void
 to fill.

It's okay
if you're not *over* someone.

If you've tried everything
and nothing seems

to work for you.

It's okay
if you don't feel

like talking about it.

If you don't feel
like dealing with it

If you don't feel
like dealing with it

right now.

It's okay
if you spent the last few months
soul searching.

But didn't find anything
while doing so.

It's okay
if you don't love them
anymore.

If you out grew
someone you thought

you'd be with forever.

If you feel
the need to move on.

It's okay
if it *still hurts.*

If you haven't grown much.
Because you know

it takes time.
It takes guts.

It's okay

if you don't feel
like getting out of bed today.

If you missed work
just to have an extra twenty-four hours

to yourself.

Twenty-four hours to listen.
To feel.

To figure out
what it is

you really want to do.

It's okay
if you haven't healed.

If some days you feel
strong and brave.

While other times
you feel fragile and weak.

It's okay
to be yourself.

To feel comfortable
in your own skin.

To say
what you want to say.

As long as it's
the truth

even if you
regret it

a few moments later.

It's okay
to break apart.

Okay to feel
a little lost.

Okay to not
know who you are.

It's okay
if yesterday you were
someone else.

If today you feel
closer to whom

you'd like to be.

It's okay.
It really is.

Some of these things take time.

And this is what it takes.
This is how you bloom.

How you begin
to put the pieces together.

This is how
it'll make sense.

How you'll find
what you love.

*How you'll chase
what you love.*

And remember,
it's okay

to change your mind
every so often.

But never change
what is in your heart.

Always stay true
to your heart.

Always

pay attention to it.

It's not okay
to ignore it.

Trust it.

It knows the way.
Never give up on it.

*Always choose to do
what you feel.*

SEARCHING

We are all searching.

Some of us for a sign.
Some of us for the right words.

For the right moment.
For the right person.

We are all searching.

And some of us
spend a lifetime doing so.

Some of us
find it early on in life.

Some of us
throughout the middle.

And some of us
never quite find

that *thing*
that speaks to us.

That book
that changes our lives.

That speech
that impact's your soul.

That one person
who inspires us

to do good.

Some of us go on
to find what we love.

Some of us get lucky
and what we love
finds us.

Finds you.

And sometimes
in the most unusual of places.

We are all searching.

Some of us never reach
our full potential.

Some of us soar high.
To new heights.

To new places.
To new worlds
and dimensions.

Some of us die too young.
Some of us

live long enough
to watch everything you love
pass on.

We are all searching.

Some of us
for the right person to hold.

For the right hands.
For the right warmth.

The right comfort.
The right softness.

While some of us search
and search

and always come up short.
Never quite finding

the right one.

The right kind of love
to hold on to.

We are all searching.

Some of us blindly.
Some of us cautiously.

Some of us
full of anticipation.

Full of love.
Full of sadness.

Full of hope and dreams.

Full of brokenness.
Emptiness.

Happiness.
And sometimes even
full of light.

We are all searching.

Searching.
Searching.
Searching.

I hope we find
what we're looking for.

I hope we don't
have to search long enough.

I hope we don't spend

our entire lives
waiting,

searching,
for the things we deserve.

For the things
we need

in order to love.

I hope life is easy
on all of us.

Forgiving.
Merciful.

I hope we find
what is meant for us.

And I hope
it's beautiful enough

to ease
the pain.

DO YOU

"Do you write
all of your material, he said."

"Of course I do.
My soul is old, man.

I feel like
I've lived for a thousand years.

Like I've gone
through a thousand heartaches.

A thousand people.
A thousand lives.

I don't know
what to do

with all of this
intensity I feel.

I don't know
how to let it out.

I lose my shit sometimes.
My cool.

I can't control it.

Sometimes I let it get
the best of me.

Sometimes it hurts.

I'm an old soul.
I let it out of my chest.

I tell it how it is.
No filter.

No preservatives.
No pesticides.

No junk.

All raw.
All heart.
All soul.
All feelings.

I try to keep it true.
I try to keep it

as real
as it can get."

FEEDING SOULS

I don't understand
why people leave people.

Especially
when they need them
the most.

How people
could just walk out,

while the one they're leaving
is breaking apart.

I don't get it.

Some people are assholes.
They only stay

if it benefits them.

They only love
if they get something
out of it.

They only care
if it feeds their souls.

WEEPING

You don't get closure
from the people

who've done you wrong.

From the people
who've left you empty,
alone and broken.

Sometimes
you have to let things be.

You have to
leave them

in the past and move on.

You shouldn't have to wait
for an apology.

For someone
to come to your aid.

For someone
to help you

make sense
of your hurting.

Sometimes
you have to learn

how to move on—on
your own.

At your pace.

Sometimes
you have to learn

how to hold your own hand
and take your own advice.

You have to do this sometimes.

It's a part of growing up.
I hope you understand

that pain
isn't forever.

That it's not there
to last

but to teach you.

To show you
what you deserve.

What to weep over.

And who to really
move on from.

Pain is a teacher.
You are a student.

And the curriculum is everlasting.

TOXIC WASTE

You can choose
to stay in your toxic relationship.

Choose to live
with what hurts.

With the disrespect.
With the pain.

With the lies.
With the same ol' story.

Or you can learn
to move on.

Learn to stand up
for yourself.

To stop making excuses.
To let them go.

To live for yourself
and heal.

This is a decision
only you can make.

A choice

only you can choose from.

You can let yourself die
or let yourself breathe.

Let yourself live.

The choice is yours.
Every day

is a new day
to start over.

A new day
to begin a new chapter

in your life.

A new adventure.
A new life.

Love.
Friendship.

And your story can either be
a sad, destructive one.

Or it can be
a beautiful one.

Based on growth.

On healing.
On moving forward.

The choice is yours.
And the choice

will always
belong to you.

IMPORTANT TO ME

It meant a lot to me.

That's why
it's been hard to move on.

Hard to get away.
To start over.

You were everything to me.
I loved you.

And I was willing
to work things out.

I was willing
to go through hell
and back.

If it meant
making it all work

in the end—staying together.

I was willing
to let myself go

for you.

Willing

to be with you
forever.

You were *that*
important to me.

BEST ROAD

I can tell you one thing.

Right now
it's going to hurt.

And it's your right
to hurt.

It's okay to do so.

From here
on out

it's not going to be
perfect.

It's not going to be
pretty.

It's going to be hard
to move on.

Hard
to get over your past.

But I will tell you this.

To trust the process.

To trust your healing.
Your lessons learned.

They are essential.

They are beautiful.
You'll learn.
You'll grow.

And it will also take
some time.

Maybe a month.
Maybe two

or even three.

But just know
that everything will work

itself out
in the end.

You will get back
on your feet.

You will build
yourself back up again.

And stronger
than before as well.

You'll see how
with time

things won't hurt
as much.

Things won't eat you alive.
You know.

But for now
they will and it sucks.

I know.

No one wants
to go through this.

But sometimes
you have to—to grow.

To learn what's right
for you—what's not.

Just take it
day by day.

Hour by hour.

Take as much time
as you need.

Believe me.

Let a few months past
down the road

and you'll see,

 how *ALL* of this
was for the best.

THE LAST

My last relationship taught me
how to value myself

before anyone else.

How to not beg
for someone's love

that love
and attraction will happen

naturally.

That is,
if it's there

from the beginning.

It taught me
how to not lower my standards.

How to not lower
my beliefs.

My feelings.
And my love for no one.

It taught me

to not chase those who don't
want to be chased.

To not waste my love
on those who don't need it.

Who don't want it.

Who don't appreciate it
the way it's meant

to be appreciated.

My last relationship taught me
so much about myself.

About the things
I need to work on.

The things
I need to learn

how to control.

How to let go.
It taught me how to find

the things I deserve.
The things that make my life

complete.

It taught me about people.
Not just love.

Not just how
to love them either.

But also,
how to be there for them.

How to talk to them.
How to listen.

How to support them
when they need it most.

How to communicate with them
when I have nothing left

to say.

My last relationship taught me a lot.
But apart from everything

I learned.

It also taught me
that learning about myself

and people
is a lifelong process.

That I will always have something
to look forward to.

Something new to discover.

Like love
I, too, need practice.

I, too, need constant
attending to myself

and my needs.

I'm more than just
a human being.

More than just
a person who needs love.

More than just
a person who is constantly

searching.

I'm my own universe.
And I'm constantly changing.

Shifting.
Transitioning.

And I don't need

the approval
of no one.

I don't need anyone's validation
to grow

the way I want
to grow.

PROTECT YOU

I know things
haven't been too easy

for you.

And I know
whatever it is

you're holding inside
gravitates toward sadness

more than anything
else.

I can see it in
your eyes.

I can see this heaviness
pouring out of your pupils.

This sad color
flowing out of them.

I know you don't
want to talk about it.

I know it might
reopen the wound.

Take you back
to that place

you've been trying
to put behind you.

I know it's hard.
Really *fucking hard*

to move on.

I know it still hurts.
I know it still

haunts you
when you're alone.

All of it, too.

From the beginning
to the end.

I know you're heart
is still broken.

I know
because I've been collecting
the pieces

you've been leaving behind.

And I've been placing them
together for you.

I know the slightest things
make you remember.

Make you fall deeper
into the void

you've created.

I know all of these things
aren't the easiest

to deal with.

But I am telling you
that there is no need

for you to cage yourself up.

There is no need
for you to go through this

alone.

No need
for you to believe

that your sadness

is *your* doom.

That what you feel inside
right now

will be the only thing
you feel

forever.

There is no need
for any of that.

No need
to pretend that you're okay.

You can be vulnerable
with me.

Cry if you want to.
Fall apart

if you must.

But please
there is no need

to do it alone.

No need
to isolate yourself

from the people
who really care.

I'm here.
And I am with you.

Thick and thin.
Fire and ice.

Hell and heaven.

I am here.
I am here.
I am here.

Therefore, you shouldn't be so quick
to close out all of the people

you love.

A best friend will always
be there for you.

Will always protect you
 no matter what.

I hope you remember this.
I hope you don't forget

how much I care.

Printed by Amazon Italia Logistica S.r.l.
Torrazza Piemonte (TO), Italy